Sir Isaac Newton in his **black** and **gold** waistcoat

Tommy Brock in his **orange** waistcoat

The gentlemen rabbits in their **grey** hats

ally Henny-penny
her **yellow** stockings

ld Mrs. Mouse and her children in the **turquoise** shoe

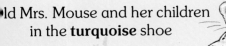

Peter Rabbit's
COLORS

With new reproductions from the original illustrations by

BEATRIX POTTER

F. WARNE & C.º ™

blue

Peter Rabbit's jacket
is **blue**

blue

"It was a blue jacket with brass buttons, quite new."
From *The Tale of Peter Rabbit*

Flopsy, Mopsy and Cotton-tail's cloaks are **red**

red

"Flopsy, Mopsy, and Cotton-tail, who were good little bunnies,
went down the lane to gather blackberries."
From *The Tale of Peter Rabbit*

Sally Henny-penny's stockings
are yellow

"That's a pair of stockings belonging to Sally Henny-penny –
look how she's worn the heels out with scratching in the yard."

From *The Tale of Mrs. Tiggy-Winkle*

green

Samuel Whiskers' coat
is **green**

green

"Mother, Mother!" said Mittens, "there has been an old man
rat in the dairy – a dreadful 'normous big rat."
From *The Tale of Samuel Whiskers*

Tabitha Twitchit's dress
is **purple**

purple

"One day Mrs. Tabitha Twitchit expected friends to tea;
so she fetched the kittens indoors, to wash and dress them."

From *The Tale of Tom Kitten*

orange

Tommy Brock's waistcoat

is orange

orange

"Tommy Brock's clothes were very dirty; and as he slept
in the day-time, he always went to bed in his boots."
From *The Tale of Mr. Tod*

brown

Peter Rabbit's shoes
are **brown**

brown

"It was the second little jacket and pair of shoes
that Peter had lost in a fortnight."
From *The Tale of Peter Rabbit*

pink

Miss Moppet's bow
is **pink**

"This is a Pussy called Miss Moppet,
she thinks she has heard a mouse!"
From *The Story of Miss Moppet*

turquoise

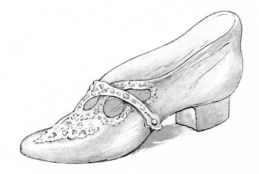

Old Mrs. Mouse's shoe
is **turquoise**

"You know the old woman
who lived in a shoe?"
From *Appley Dapply's Nursery Rhymes*

grey

The gentlemen rabbits' hats
are **grey**

grey

Two gentlemen rabbits walking in the snow.

From *Appley Dapply's Nursery Rhymes*

black

Sir Isaac Newton's waistcoat
is **black** and gold

gold

"His friends both came to dinner. Sir Isaac Newton wore his black and gold waistcoat."

From *The Tale of Mr. Jeremy Fisher*

Framingham State College
Framingham, Massachusetts

Peter Rabbit's mother's
pocket-handkerchief
is **red** and white

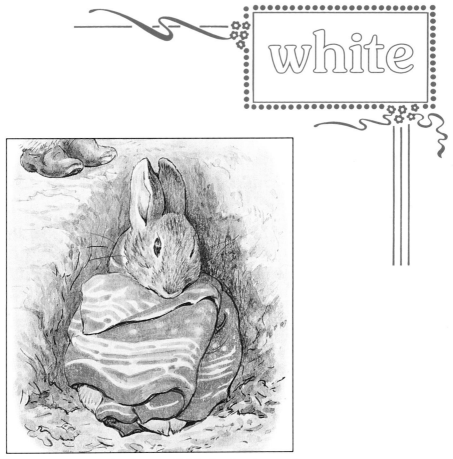

"Peter was sitting by himself. He looked poorly,
and was dressed in a red cotton pocket-handkerchief."
From *The Tale of Peter Rabbit*

blue

Jemima Puddle-duck's shawl
is **blue** and **pink**

pink

"She set off on a fine spring afternoon.
She was wearing a shawl and a poke bonnet."
From *The Tale of Jemima Puddle-Duck*

"Now I've finished my ironing: I'm going to air some clothes."
From *The Tale of Mrs. Tiggy-Winkle*

Mrs. Tiggy-Winkle washes and irons all the animals' clothes.

"And she hung up all sorts and sizes of clothes."
From *The Tale of Mrs Tiggy-Winkle*

Then she hangs them up to air.

Can you remember the colors?

FREDERICK WARNE
Published by the Penguin Group
27 Wrights Lane, London W8 5TZ, England
Viking Penguin Inc., 40 West 23rd Street, New York, New York 10010, USA
Penguin Books Australia Ltd, Ringwood, Victoria, Australia
Penguin Books Canada Ltd, 2801 John Street, Markham, Ontario, Canada L3R 1B4
Penguin Books (NZ) Ltd, 182-190 Wairau Road, Auckland 10, New Zealand

Penguin Books Ltd, Registered Offices: Harmondsworth, Middlesex, England

First published 1988

ISBN 0 7232 3551 1

Printed and bound in Great Britain by William Clowes Limited,
Beccles and London

Flopsy, Mopsy and Cotton-tail
in their **red** cloaks

Jemima Puddle-duck in
blue and **pink** shawl

Peter Rabbit in his **blue** jacket
and **brown** shoes

Miss Moppet in
her **pink** bow

Samuel Whiskers in
his **green** coat

Benjamin Bunny with the
red and **white** pocket-handkerch

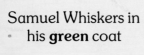